McQUEEN

UEEN

THE ILLUSTRATED HISTORY
OF A FASHION ICON

Written by
Tom Rasmussen

Illustrated by
R. Song

Smith
Street
Books

INTRODUCTION

Lee Alexander McQueen

Lee Alexander McQueen was, and remains, one of the greatest fashion designers the world has ever seen. In his relatively short career, McQueen – like all the design greats – pushed the boundaries of fashion, transforming the industry. He melded fashion and technology, he challenged his audiences, he found beauty in the most unexpected of places, and all the while, he made the world watch.

On the eve of 'Plato's Atlantis', his final show before his death, his producer tried on the famous Armadillo boots – the 10-inch heels that became a signature shape for the McQueen brand – and she couldn't walk. She ran to find Lee and explained the problem, worried about the models. He simply replied, 'If they fall, they fall.'

Nobody fell. His producer, Sam Gainsbury, later told *The Guardian*, 'Before the show Lee was backstage with all these 17-year-old models, looking into their eyes, telling them how incredible they looked, how proud he was [of them], that they could do it. He gave them such confidence. And not one of them fell. It was like a gift, with Lee. He made you feel like you were capable of anything.'

Featuring an appearance from Lady Gaga, who premiered her new single during the show, 'Plato's Atlantis' was the first runway show ever to be streamed live from the catwalk. Instead of going down in history as a tale of tumbling models, it became known as fashion's vision of the future – both in terms of the printed, intricately constructed reptilian garments, and in its depiction of how fashion and technology could work together to expand fashion's audience. Suddenly the exclusive world of fashion wasn't just for those who had a front-row seat – everyone was invited.

Now we see this phenomenon everywhere – the democratisation of the catwalk, some might call it – allowing people who had never before had access to a fashion show the chance to get up close and personal to what was happening on the runway. And it was McQueen's boldness in questioning what fashion should be, and who it should be for, that brought about this industry-altering shift.

That's how he approached fashion – as though it was capable of anything. Countless testimonies exist, from those who worked closely with McQueen to those who met him once, all depicting his optimism when it came to design: there was nothing that wasn't possible, and McQueen proved this on the runway time and time again.

But beyond his incontestable fashion genius, he was a man full of complexities, living in both darkness and light. He was troubled but sweet, acerbic but deeply loving, an addict, a comedian, a pessimist and an optimist.

While McQueen's designs keep him on the lips and mood-boards of so many people today, his personality, his attitude, and his unlikely position as a working-class boy from East London heralded as the rebel king of fashion, only enhances this legacy – a legacy that is as dark as it is inspiring.

This book is an illustrated view into McQueen's remarkable life and work. It's a celebration of the man and the fashion designer who left fashion, and the world, a little more complex, a little more beautiful, and a little more challenging than he found it.

01—

YOUTH & EDUCATION

YOUTH & EDUCATION

Lee McQueen was the unlikely trailblazer who changed fashion forever. From a working-class background in East London, McQueen's start in life did not feature glamorous women, high fashion or a focus on art and creativity. Famous for finding beauty in the most unexpected of places, it was at home in the working-class streets of Stratford where McQueen developed his eye for drama, darkness, and twisted splendour.

After a tricky time at secondary school, McQueen went from fashion apprentice to design assistant, finally landing a place in the design masters at the revered fashion school, Central Saint Martins. The minute he sent his graduation collection down the runway, he fell into favour with one of fashion's greats – Isabella Blow.

Lee Alexander McQueen, Britain's former reigning king of fashion, was born in Lewisham, East London on 17 March, 1969. The youngest son of Joyce, a school teacher, and Ronald, a taxi driver, McQueen started life in a small council flat, among a block of postwar standard-issue houses, eventually moving to a terraced house in nearby Stratford.

Less imaginative people would find little inspiration among the brutalist brick and concrete of East London, but McQueen spent his early years gazing at the birds of prey that circled the railway tracks and telephone masts that populate the landscape of East London's industrial heart. These majestic birds, amid their rigid settings, would later come to inform much of McQueen's design aesthetic, and influence his talent for creating beauty from the most meagre and unexpected of things.

In the '70s and '80s, East London wasn't the gentrified creative hub it is now. The streets were much more aggressive, crime was rife, and creativity and flamboyancy weren't met with reward. 'It's an honest place. If someone's gonna mug you they tell you before they do it,' McQueen once remarked. His love of dark beauty was born here, against a backdrop of brown and red brick and steelwork.

In the early years of his life, Lee shared a small room with his two brothers. Despite his humble beginnings, McQueen had big plans. He announced his dreams of being a fashion designer at a very young age, while attending Carpenters Primary School near his home. He would spend his days draping his sister in bed sheets and curtains he found lying around, making her model for him, bringing to life his first fashion creations.

Known for making garments move, it was here McQueen's eye for draping and skill in manipulating fabric began: at home, his older sister his muse. But for a young boy from a working-class background, these dreams were unlikely to come true. The fashion world is a long way from Stratford, and the elite and nepotistic circles of this milieu seem impenetrable for those from less-privileged backgrounds.

After primary school, Lee attended Rokeby School in Canning Town, a boys' school where his flamboyant character was often met with homophobic sneers of 'McQueer'. An awkward, imaginative teenager, he struggled to make friends with his classmates.

And while a young McQueen still dreamed of fashion, he left school at sixteen with one qualification in art – an academic record that was unlikely to lead him to the dizzying heights of fashion success. His time at high school remains undiscussed, but like many creative geniuses, McQueen's youth was punctuated with bullying and misunderstanding.

Just after Lee quit school, his mum saw a news report about the shortage of apprentices skilled enough to work on Savile Row. Knowing he had always been passionate about fashion, she persuaded him to apply for a position assisting London's tailoring masters.

So, after quitting school in 1986, McQueen's eye for fabric earned him an apprenticeship on Savile Row with Cornelius O'Callaghan – a brilliant coat maker who preferred his assistants to have no fashion training, because that meant they had fewer ideas, and were much easier to train. McQueen was perfect.

The streets of Mayfair are lined by men and women with pockets of gold, and McQueen found himself in the heart of the world's foremost home of fine tailoring, frequented by royalty, aristocracy and the richest subset of the world's population. It was during his first post at the royally appointed tailor Anderson & Sheppard that McQueen imbibed everything there was to know about cutting patterns, tailoring, padding, and building bespoke tailored suits to fit the bodies of the highest paying customers. Not only was he incredibly skilled, he was also an incredibly quick learner.

Before long a young McQueen was creating made-to-measure garments for royalty, most notably Prince Charles. 'I'm in Savile Row, at the top of this old building with all these old tailors and it was Prince Charles' jacket I'm working on,' McQueen once explained in a documentary, 'and I draw this big willy on it.' From the word go, Lee's relationship with fashion was one of sabotage and tradition, seeing fashion as a means of expression. Even in a role as uninspiring as a tailor on Savile Row, Lee found a way to subvert the rules and question the hierarchies upon which big institutions are built. Lee would carry this attitude with him throughout his career, and his work would eventually question the very seams upon which fashion and its surrounding industry was sewn.

Lee's personal life was a far cry from the shining streets of Savile Row. By night, Lee and his friends would flood the streets of Soho, London's gay district. Here was a world that would come to constantly inform McQueen's designs. Full of drugs, poverty, prostitution, sex, alcohol, and night after night of dancing, laughing and loving, Soho was where many of Lee's integral personal relationships would blossom. 'There's always an energy in London: the poverty, the unemployment, the drug-induced environment, the nightlife ...' said Lee. He loved it.

After McQueen completed his apprenticeship at Anderson & Sheppard, he moved two doors down to esteemed tailors Gieves & Hawkes, but swiftly tired of the monotony of tailoring the same thing for the richest of the rich. 'I knew I couldn't survive in a place like that for the rest of my life,' McQueen said. 'Cluttered in a small workshop, padding lapels. But I was good at it: I could tailor a jacket very quickly. I was quick at learning ... And I wanted to learn everything.'

McQueen eventually left Gieves & Hawkes, and moved 'down the Row' – to Berman and Nathans – where he took up a role in the pattern-cutting department, learning to cut intricate lines in the most expensive fabric.

After his time on Savile Row, a twenty-year-old McQueen moved a little further west – to Notting Hill – to the house of heralded designer Koji Tatsuno, as a pattern cutter. McQueen was in his element for a time: working for the house that was globally famed for taking vintage fabrics and reworking them into contemporary, expressive, exciting women's clothes. But fashions change, as does the revenue a company brings in, and a downsize in the middle of a financial recession saw McQueen made redundant and unsure where to head next.

"

I ALWAYS WANTED TO BE A DESIGNER.

I   READ   BOOKS
ON   FASHION   FROM
THE   AGE   OF   12.

"

So, like anyone with fashion nous, he persuaded his sister, a travel agent, to book him a one-way ticket to Milan. 'The biggest thing at that time was Romeo Gigli,' McQueen explained. 'He was everywhere. I thought, this is the only person I want to work for. I was twenty years old. I walked into Romeo Gigli with the worst portfolio you've ever seen, full of costume design. They said they had nothing for me and that they'd call me if anything came up. Anyway, I was walking down the street afterwards and this girl came screaming up to me like a madwoman: "Stop, stop, stop, Romeo wants to see you. He wants to see you tomorrow. Come back."'

Gigli took a shine to Lee, who quickly started pattern cutting for the Milanese house. Some years later, Romeo Gigli would recount a story that captured McQueen's anti-establishment attitude towards rules: when working on a new jacket style for the designer, Lee was asked to remake it three times. After the third try, Gigli took apart the jacket, only to find the words 'Fuck you' scrawled on the inner lining.

McQueen returned to London armed with a technical knowledge that would rival the most skilled makers in the industry. He'd learned the need for precision from Savile Row, complex pattern cutting during a short stint at Bermans & Nathans, expressive construction at Koji Tatsuno, and the importance of pace and perfection at Romeo Gigli. But equally important to all this skill was McQueen's energy, his outlook, and his friends. It was the collision of Lee's impressive technical skill and outrageous personal life that would enable him to create fashion visions nobody had ever imagined possible – McQueen included.

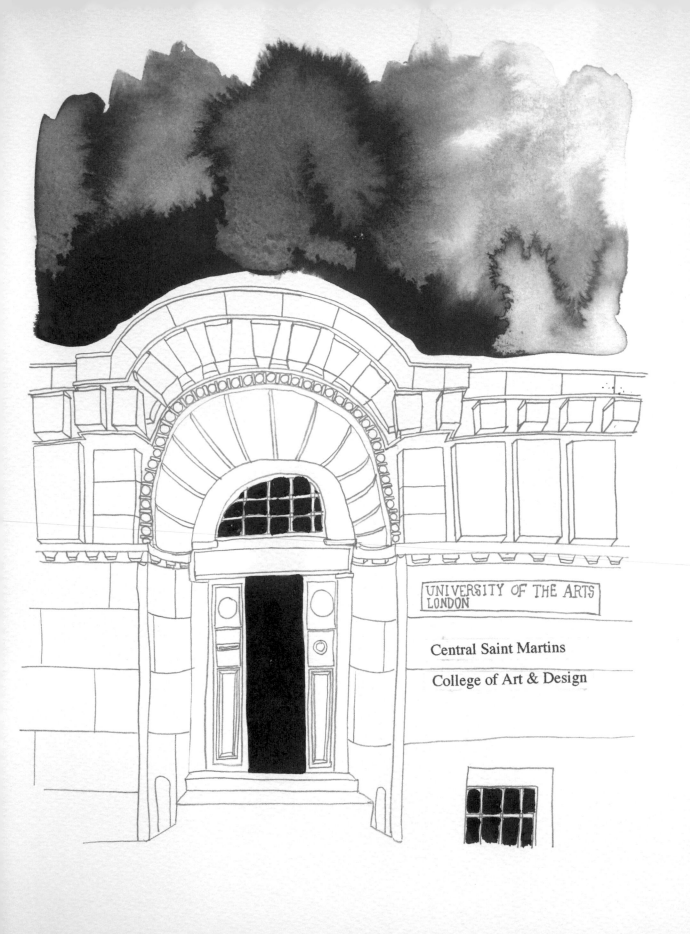

By late 1990 McQueen was twenty-one, broke and out of work. While trawling for jobs in the trade, he saw an ad for a position teaching pattern cutting at the world-renowned art and design school at Central Saint Martins. Bobby Hillson, the Fashion Masters course director at the time, found McQueen loitering outside her door. She asked him what he wanted, and he answered, 'A job'. Bobby knew that the students would never take Lee seriously as he was the same age as them, and didn't give him the job. But she did start to talk to him about the Fashion MA. Fascinated by his energy, she asked him to come back with samples of his tailoring and his drawings.

Hillson later reflected in documentary *McQueen and I* that she'd thought, 'He probably won't last. He probably won't be able to take it. Because all the others [students] had come up through the right routes.' But, lo and behold, McQueen enrolled in the Fashion MA course at Central Saint Martins, and spent the year impressing his once-dubious teachers.

This was perhaps the biggest turning point in McQueen's life to date. Now, instead of being within the structure of a brand, he was to be the brand – creating his own vision from start to finish. Nobody would be asking him to remake something, to cut it differently, or to avoid profane or subversive references. And, for the first time, against the odds, this working-class young gay man from East London had started making his childhood dreams come true.

As the runway shows for the students' graduate collections rolled around, the fashion press clamoured to see what Central Saint Martins' class of '92 would bring to the fashion forum. For many, this show is the most exposure their work will ever get, but McQueen's graduate runway set him on a direct path to stardom. The extraordinary Isabella Blow, contributing fashion stylist at *Vogue* magazine, was looking on from the steps of the venue. Blow was fashion dynamite, and she would go on to become McQueen's biggest champion.

'The pieces went past me, and they moved in a way I'd never seen,' Blow remarked of Lee's graduate collection, entitled 'Jack the Ripper Stalks His Victims', in which long silk coats in pink, black and red fluttered down the runway. Each piece had a lock of McQueen's hair bonded between two pieces of acrylic on the inside: representing the old tradition of giving hair to a lover as a token, often purchased from prostitutes rather than cut from their own hair.

Little did Blow or McQueen know that their meeting would change both their lives irrevocably. Blow was smitten with the collection, calling and calling McQueen's home phone from her office at *Vogue*. After almost twenty phone calls, McQueen finally returned one. There and then she offered him £5000 for his entire graduate collection. He said yes.

02—

ALEXANDER & ISSIE

ALEXANDER & ISSIE

Lee McQueen and Isabella Blow formed the world's most renowned fashion friendship. Issie dubbed him Alexander, and Alexander brought Issie's fashion dreams to life. Together, the pair were prolific, their relationship tumultuous, and their legacy tremendous.

Alexander & Issie

"

HE'S A WILD BIRD WITH A GOOD SILHOUETTE. BIRDS HAVE MOVEMENT, THEY HAVE FREEDOM, THEY'RE WILD, THEY'RE FREE. THEY DON'T HAVE TO BE RESPONSIBLE TO ANYONE EXCEPT THEIR GREAT TECHNICAL ABILITY TO FLY. AND HE MAKES CLOTHES FLY.

"

– Isabella Blow on Alexander McQueen

Isabella Blow was one of fashion's last true eccentrics. She was known in the fashion community for her true lust for style, and for her utter dedication to living a life surrounded by beauty. In McQueen, Isabella found boundless beauty in the most unlikely of places: a chubby, working-class lad from East London.

It was love at first sight. In February 1992, when Blow failed to get a seat at McQueen's virtuoso Saint Martins' graduate show, she opted for a seat on the floor instead.

MCQUEEN

Issie became obsessed. She was so drawn by the darkness, the 'flesh and blood' in McQueen's graduate collection that she was determined to buy the entire collection outright before anyone else could. 'The next day I rang up, and I couldn't get hold of him,' Blow explained. 'His mother said to Alexander, "There's this madwoman who keeps trying to call us. She wants some of your clothes." I rang between six and eight times a day. Finally, I got a little voice at the end of the line.'

That little voice was McQueen's, and he agreed to sell Blow the collection. In the true style of English aristocrats, she was dead broke, so each week Blow and McQueen would stop at different ATMs across London, where she would withdraw £100 in return for a black bin bag full of pieces from McQueen's collection. Already confident in his skill, McQueen wouldn't haggle, and the pair continued this 'buy now pay later' scheme until Blow had coughed up the promised £5000.

This sealed their relationship. In Issie, Lee had found an unlikely muse, his first patron, and his biggest champion. And in Lee, Issie had found someone to nurture, to mother, and to influence.

Together, the pair took the fashion industry by storm. It was like an explosion: rock met roll, and everyone was hooked. McQueen's designs and Blow's attitude both possessed a rawness that was perfect for fashion at the time. It caused shock and dismay across this world, but it kept people coming back, time after time, to witness the next spectacle. Blow once described fashion as sabotage and tradition, and both Blow and McQueen utterly personified this.

Soon it was time for McQueen's first post-graduation collection, a gritty, blood-splattered homage to the brilliant movie *Taxi Driver*. For this next show, McQueen was one of six designers invited by the British Fashion Council to exhibit at The Ritz hotel. Blow and McQueen had become a fashion force, and stories later surfaced of how Blow tore through the corridors of The Ritz, dragging all her fashion friends to the showroom to lay eyes on the 'next big thing'. And boy, was she right.

MCQUEEN

By this time, McQueen had undergone perhaps his most important rebranding: changing his name from Lee to Alexander – his middle name. 'Everyone else calls him Lee. I call him Alexander, because of Alexander the Great,' was Isabella's reasoning. In McQueen she had found a platonic soulmate, a person she could support and encourage. She offered him access to all manner of things, from her country house to her little black book of big fashion contacts.

'He was chubby, smiley, beautiful,' Issie once said of McQueen. Blow would invite McQueen to go to her country pile, Hilles, where she lived with her husband Detmar. During downtime, Blow ensured McQueen had plenty to keep him occupied. She would organise lavish dinners, and falconry lessons with birds like those McQueen grew up watching – but these ones responded to his call and came to his wrist.

"

THE PIECES WENT
PAST ME AND THEY
MOVED IN A WAY I
HAD NEVER SEEN AND
I WANTED THEM.

I JUST KNEW HE HAD
S O M E T H I N G
REALLY   SPECIAL,
VERY MODERN, IT WAS
ABOUT   SABOTAGE
AND   TRADITION.

"

Alexander & Issie

Blow's glorious country manor would become a home away from home for an increasingly successful McQueen, a kind of den of delights and revelry. Issie and McQueen were close friends for over fifteen years, despite experiencing many bumps along the way, and at Hilles the pair spent countless nights drinking, taking drugs and talking into the small hours, until McQueen eventually retired to the palatial Long Room, reserved for Blow's esteemed guests. McQueen would go to Hilles for extended periods: to rest, to work, to escape London or Paris, to shoot clay pigeons, to simply look to nature for inspiration.

But Issie's influence went deeper than extravagant pleasures and countryside inspirations, extending to brilliant contacts and remarkable press coverage, which helped McQueen achieve unprecedented industry success very early on. Within the first few years of McQueen's career, Blow had featured his work in a giant spread in *The Face* magazine, and had modelled for *Vogue* wearing head-to-toe McQueen. This was an accolade unheard of for a designer just starting out. But Blow adored McQueen like her own child – and she loved his clothes even more.

At every McQueen show, there were always two people who stood up the whole time in utter joy and support for Lee: his mum, and Issie. Even when McQueen eventually took the reins at the storied Parisian fashion house Givenchy, which caused bad blood with Blow, she still sat front row and applauded every look that came down the runway.

Within three years of meeting the pair had conquered London and initiated a brand-new wave of brilliant Britannia. The world began looking to London for innovative, exciting answers to fashion's questions. This period is still known as one of the most riveting times in fashion, a period people often try to replicate, though nobody has succeeded yet.

Alexander & Issie

72

Lee and Issie's relationship was constantly being reimagined in new formats: Isabella as muse, confidante, patron, mother, and press manager. For McQueen's 1994 show 'Banshee', Blow even offered herself up as a model. Held at the once-iconic Café de Paris in London's Piccadilly, the unlikely model graced the runway in a lace dress, waistcoat and a high-collared shirt in a regal purple. Issie's hair was lacquered flat to her face, and McQueen's surname was intricately lettered across her idiosyncratic jet-black bob in bright silver. Issie's turn on the runway was met with cheers and applause from her many friends and admirers, and when she appeared in her second outfit she famously paused and took another lap around the runway, loving every moment.

Stories like these populate the colourful, outrageous, absurd history of fashion's favourite friendship. Now that the gates to the fashion crowd had been smashed open by McQueen with Issie at his side, the industry became populated with a far more diverse crowd. The misfits had risen to power, and fast: by 1997 Givenchy were on the hunt for a new creative director to replace the other London-trained legend, John Galliano. By this time, McQueen had gained such momentum he'd become a hurricane. And so, just six years after McQueen presented his graduate collection, he was the only option for Givenchy. A post usually taken by a master was now filled by a rebel.

This was it! McQueen was, once again, on the up, and his number one supporter and muse, after a much longer life in fashion, would finally be rewarded with a well-paid position and, most importantly, a true creative role in making fashion.

GIVENCHY

When the contracts were signed with Givenchy, the pair celebrated over caviar and champagne. But to Issie's dismay, she was nowhere to be seen in the deal. In a move that shocked both the industry and Issie herself, Lee had purposefully omitted her and left Issie to hear of her exclusion from others. Many said that the friendship never quite recovered. Issie took herself back to London, heartbroken and betrayed, while McQueen set up shop in the Givenchy studios in Paris.

GIVENCHY

According to her husband Detmar, Issie was devastated, 'but the problem was Issie couldn't fall out with him because she was addicted to McQueen. She didn't want to lose the clothes.'

Instead, Blow did everything she could to support McQueen in his new role – organising shoots with prestigious photographers and models; trying to claim a €35,000 Givenchy dress as an expense on her business account at the *Sunday Times*; applauding every single look on the runway at McQueen's 'disastrous' first Givenchy show. She even turned up to one of McQueen's shows in a full dog suit and collar in the hope that he'd like it. But by 1998, even Issie had realised the changing stakes of their relationship. 'It's like vampires ... you need somebody and then you don't need the drug anymore,' she once said of McQueen's treatment of her.

While McQueen's tenure at Givenchy slowly began to blossom, Blow's journalistic career was also resuscitated after she was reappointed to her former fashion position at *Tatler*. For a few years, their paths were smooth, though they crossed less and less in the wake of one of fashion's most shocking betrayals.

A few years passed, by which time the pair shared much love but little creative collaboration. And while there was endless speculation about whether the infamous duo really cared for each other, when Blow was admitted to rehab in 2006, McQueen – who was by now incredibly well off – paid most of the fee, desperate for her to overcome the depression she had been battling for years.

Having separated from Detmar, Isabella completed her treatment and went back to Hilles to make peace with her husband. McQueen, by this point, disapproved of Isabella's relationship with Detmar, and the pair drifted apart once again.

On 7 May, 2007, the much adored, respected and revered Isabella Blow swallowed weed-killer at her home in Gloucestershire and subsequently passed away in Gloucestershire Royal Hospital. 'I'm fighting depression, and I can't beat it,' Blow told her husband Detmar. Like so many brilliant artists before her, Isabella's depression won a lifelong battle. But Blow's legacy – from the talent she discovered to the way she lived, dressed, and revelled in life – will forever live on.

McQueen never really recovered from losing Issie, one of
the great loves of his life. Five months after her passing,
McQueen and Philip Treacy – another of Blow's protégés –
staged 'Le Dame Bleu' in Paris: a fashion show in memory
of one of the few true icons fashion ever knew. Even in
her death, she remained at the heart of McQueen's work.

Journalists and editors concurred that the show was one of the most powerful, meaningful moments fashion has ever seen, with many observing that such moments transcend fashion entirely. Together, McQueen and Blow were the pair who dedicated their lives to achieving just that: transcending fashion.

'A muse is someone who is a constant inspiration,' Blow said of her relationship with McQueen. 'You can't buy a muse, it's like a love affair with somebody.' And for McQueen and Blow, however tumultuous their relationship, it really, really was.

03—

THE
COLLECTIONS

THE COLLECTIONS

McQueen's runway shows for his self-titled brand were where his imagination really came to life. This was where he redefined the limits of what fashion could be, and snatched the attention of both the fashion industry and the world. From blood to urine, birds of prey to earthworms, McQueen's daring, often outrageous approach to runway shows catapulted him to global fame and commercial success, and cemented his position as one of the most influential fashion designers in history. Spanning three major cities, McQueen's collections grew in style and scale over his twenty-year career, and his runway shows never failed to stimulate, challenge and shock their viewers.

"

I THINK THERE IS BEAUTY IN EVERYTHING. WHAT 'NORMAL' PEOPLE WOULD PERCEIVE AS UGLY, I CAN USUALLY SEE SOMETHING OF BEAUTY IN IT.

"

– Alexander McQueen

Over the course of his twenty-year career in fashion, McQueen was constantly reinventing the limits of both fashion design and fashion as theatre. Tickets to a McQueen show were like gold dust, with editors, fashion press and obsessive fans and clients alike desperate to be part of the next glorious, controversial frontier.

In fashion, people are always looking for the next 'moment'. But the very concept of a fashion moment was arguably invented by McQueen himself. Not a single show in the forty or more he designed passed by without creating yet another 'moment'.

Whatever McQueen's context, he was truly momentous. 'Give me time and I'll give you a revolution,' he once said. And he was right: he revolutionised fashion over and over again.

MA GRADUATE COLLECTION 1992 –
'Jack the Ripper Stalks His Victims'

McQueen's use of darkness in his design revealed itself
very early on. In his graduate collection, he was inspired
by Jack the Ripper, the East London killer who stalked and
murdered prostitutes during the 1880s. McQueen grew
up not far from the site of the murders – it was rumoured
that a relative of his rented a room to one of the Ripper's
victims. The collection itself is the stuff of fashion legend
now, with only a few pieces still in existence. It featured
tailored coats in dark fabrics and giant skirts with faces
printed across them, and mixed Old English Victoriana
with a sexual energy that was rare on the runway at the
time. The most famous piece is perhaps a pink silk tail
coat, covered in printed thorns.

AUTUMN/WINTER 1993 – 'Taxi Driver'

In the history of fashion, there have been very few designers who could lay claim to inventing a brand-new silhouette. But McQueen, in his second ever collection, had done just that. Apparently inspired by the builder's bum, the Bumster was tailored perfectly to bisect the body at the exact halfway point: a line on the body that had never been explored before. The only person known to own an original pair of Bumsters is the iconic princess of pop, Kylie Minogue, who ordered a pair directly from McQueen. The rest of the collection, inspired by the gritty, bloody movie *Taxi Driver*, was left in trash bags outside a club on the night of the show. The trash bags were disposed of by street cleaners while McQueen partied inside, oblivious, until the early hours of the morning.

SPRING/SUMMER 1993 –
'Theatre of Cruelty'

McQueen's second show post-graduation was considered pivotal. Now the press had gathered, and fashion folk had come to see what all the whispers were about. In a famous review, one critic remarked, 'models who look as if they have recently experienced serious traffic accidents, in sheer and sweaty clingfilm knickers, with what appeared to be bloody, suppurating, post-operative breasts visible through muslin T-shirts, was rather a lot to take in the name of frocks'. Indeed, the industry wasn't sure what to do with McQueen at this stage. It was gory, violent, bloody, but people stayed in their seats because everyone was looking for the promise of the new. Even though McQueen's shock tactics made critics feel uneasy, fashion was ready for a reimagined punk attitude, something McQueen delivered in droves. Featuring his classic Bumsters, perfectly tailored jackets in pink and flesh-tone silks that darted from the breast and revealed naked torsos, as well as blood-spattered dresses and dripping wet tees, this collection foreshadowed what was to become the McQueen signature: impeccable tailoring bolstered by an ineffably wild, dark and daring imagination.

SPRING/SUMMER 1995 – 'The Birds'

Ever inspired by birds, McQueen's collection featured what would become his signature swallow print, which lives on across his designs even today. Featuring models including a young *Vogue* editor, Plum Sykes, and the remarkably contorted, corseted Mr Pearl with his tiny cinched waist, 'The Birds' was the collection where McQueen first introduced what would eventually become the fashion house's DNA: deconstructed tailoring.

AUTUMN/WINTER 1995 – 'Highland Rape'

Always delving into history, this time exploring his Scottish heritage, 'Highland Rape' became one of McQueen's most criticised and adored collections. With some press branding it misogynistic and fetishising of violence against women, others felt it was deeply emotional and a commentary on the way women's bodies were used in warfare.

Suzy Menkes said that this was the first time she'd ever seen McQueen truly put himself into his work, and the result was astounding. Women with torn tartan dresses stumbled across the runway, in a collection inspired by the ethnic cleansing of Scottish Highland natives by British Forces in the eighteenth and nineteenth centuries. For this collection, McQueen revisited the Bumster, and tailored dresses so they would drape and fall from each model's frame perfectly and precisely.

SPRING/SUMMER 1996 –
'The Hunger'

Worms. In fashion. Actual worms, in fashion. Yes, of course that was McQueen. Referencing the erotic vampire movie *The Hunger*, models famously flipped off the audience while wearing bondage straps and perspex corsets that sealed live worms and long hairs inside them. The models were often dripping with blood and wearing casts, all while donning precisely cut and constructed tailored jackets and skin-tight pencil skirts.

AUTUMN/WINTER 1996 –
'Dante'

Always looking for the next way to shock the press, McQueen cheekily sat a skeleton in the front row for the show. Noted editors and fashion folk were greeted by the skeleton as they filed into a candlelit church in East London's Spitalfields, McQueen's chosen setting for the next of his dramatic instalments. It was in 'Dante' that Lee began to explore religious signifiers and Victoriana, an aesthetic that became a major building block in the brand's DNA. Blasphemy, beauty, brilliance.

The never-ending buzz generated by his collections made McQueen one of the first real rockstars of the fashion design world. Gone were the days of the silent genius, locked in a studio, sending demure messages through only their clothes. Although this attitude still played a huge part in McQueen's process, he had quickly risen to the top, becoming the commander-in-chief of what was cool.

People were desperate for his work, and for the rebellious status that came with it. The nineties were in full swing, and European club culture, cheap travel and cheap drugs were taking all industries to new heights. With the internet slowly starting to make sense, communication was quicker, and the closed walls of industries like fashion were being brought down by the likes of McQueen and his misfits – proving to onlookers that even the most unlikely could enter the fashion arena.

It was an exciting and bold move for the iconic Parisienne couture house Givenchy to welcome McQueen – who had graduated from university a mere six years prior – as their creative director. Until then, appointments like this simply didn't happen.

And in true McQueen style, he rose to the prestigious opportunity in the best way he knew how: with outrage and rebellion. There are endless accounts of McQueen swanning into the Givenchy atelier in Paris, taking designs that skilled craftsmen and women had worked on for weeks, and chopping them up on the mannequin in front of everyone. He caused utter dismay among the French press – who laud and protect their native design talents – after telling one journalist he thought Hubert de Givenchy, the house's founder, had no talent.

He was set for stardom. But as his first ever show on the global stage rolled around, McQueen learned what it was to fail. Journalists, editors and faithful clients felt McQueen's first offering in the couture arena was superficial, poorly thought out and gimmicky. In hindsight, McQueen thought so too, admitting in an interview that this first collection was 'crap'.

AUTUMN/WINTER 1997 –
'It's a Jungle Out There'

Hair became manes, eyes became slicked with thick black eyeliner; feral models stormed the butcher's station at Borough Market, which, back then, was a real, gritty London trade market – and a shock for the tottering editors in attendance. Inspired by HG Wells' infamous novel, *The Island of Doctor Moreau*, McQueen played a fashion vivisectionist: slicing and stitching animal skins, patched here and there to create models of half-animal, half-human appearance. Kate Moss tore down the runway like a wild predator, while audience members reportedly fainted at the overwhelming beastliness of fashion's most beautiful girls.

MCQUEEN

SPRING/SUMMER 1998 –
'The Golden Shower'/'Untitled'

While McQueen was primarily focused on exploring pain, he knew better than most just how closely pain links with pleasure. The collection's tailoring started sharp, slowly growing looser and sheerer, exposing flesh as the show went on. In the second half, golden rain fell from above, soaking the models through and exposing naked skin beneath sheer white outfits. Originally named 'The Golden Shower' – after the act of urination during sex – corporate sponsors were apparently outraged at the unadulterated sexuality of the show, and demanded a name change. Now the collection is known as 'Untitled', but who can forget a golden shower?

MCQUEEN

AUTUMN/WINTER 1998 –
'Joan'

For autumn, McQueen wanted to warm up. Moving on from cold, golden rain, this season the designer played with fire – literally. Layer upon layer of metal mesh was printed with the faces of the Romanov children. Models wore bald caps and red contact lenses. Flowing gowns were juxtaposed against dramatic red python print fabric; some models even walked in chain mail. The finale, perhaps one of McQueen's most memorable scenes, saw a model in all red encircled in flames – a reference to the Catholic martyr and feminist hero Joan of Arc. As the flames grew, so did the volume of Diana Ross's voice, bursting with the lyrics 'you're gonna make it, you're gonna make it' over an iconic disco beat.

AUTUMN/WINTER 1999 –
'The Overlook'

Inspired by classic horror films, 'The Overlook' took reference from *The Shining*, but with a twist. Many argue this show was one of McQueen's most poetic, staged in a giant lucite snow globe, with giant shearling coats, huge hand knits and intricate patchworking. Ice skaters peppered the Victorian scene. This was emblematic of McQueen's most important skills: to dream up shows of pure beauty, featuring clothes that were, ultimately, wearable and sellable. This was McQueen's genius formula, which so few before or after him could achieve.

SPRING/SUMMER 2000 –
'Eye'

McQueen moved stateside for his first collection post the turn of the millennium. The whole fashion industry trekked far from the centre of Manhattan, to a huge warehouse on the West Side pier, to witness what genius McQueen might dream up in this new American context. As ever, it was drama from start to finish. Models waded through what appeared to be black water, in a show that mixed sportswear, sex and Middle Eastern references. The show featured a powerhouse Gisele in an embroidered head covering and metal bodysuit, stomping down the runway, all-powerful in McQueen's creations. Slowly, spikes rose through the water, setting the audience on the edge of their seats as acrobats dangled above thousands of sharp metal points, performing dances in red and black burqa-like outfits. Ever the showman, the runway presentation climaxed with McQueen dropping his trousers, revealing boxer shorts plastered with stars and stripes.

AUTUMN/WINTER 2000 –
'Eshu'

Back to London and McQueen's favoured theme of Victoriana, this time married with Nigerian influence in the form of Yoruba neck rings. Björk would begin her long-term artistic relationship with the designer here, going on to be photographed in an acid-wash hoop dress that was very in sync with the trends of the noughties.

While producing his shows for his own Alexander McQueen label, Lee was still at Givenchy, where he remained for four years, happily making a profit for the label with his subsequent collections. It became evident over the time he was at Givenchy that his energies were better spent on his home turf in London, where his eponymous brand had continued to flourish. After his first collection at Givenchy, McQueen had begun to play ball, incorporating the traditional house codes into collections which he aimed at a younger client. But it was at his Alexander McQueen label, less penned in by rules and regulations, that McQueen produced radical collections like 'Joan', 'The Overlook', and 'Eye' – and where people still got their true McQueen fix.

In 2000, when the Gucci group appointed designer Tom Ford to invest in fashion houses around the world, top of his list was, of course, Alexander McQueen. Within months the deal was done, and McQueen had sold 51 per cent of his company to the global giant – and the main competitor of LVMH, who owned Givenchy.

While French houses have always favoured the brilliance of British designers, they've never shied away from cutting ties to them, either – as evidenced in the termination of McQueen's tenure at Givenchy after news of the Gucci deal broke. His final show at Givenchy was stripped of its production, and shown in two quiet sittings to a select group of editors and buyers totalling less than ninety people.

Even though McQueen's time at Givenchy is often seen as a side-note in his creative archive, Givenchy had brought him to a global audience – an audience that followed McQueen back to London, where he now had more budget, more production, and more vigour than ever. It was the millennium, and it was a new dawn for McQueen.

SPRING/SUMMER 2001 –
'Voss'

If any show cemented McQueen as the king of fashion theatre, it was 'Voss'. A truly monumental work in McQueen's oeuvre, attendees were seated in a mirrored box, staring at their own reflection for nearly an hour before the show began. The lights flickered on, revealing the insides of this enclosure: a psychiatric ward of sorts, housing yet another box in the centre. Models flitted through the doors and into the space, writhing and squirming, wearing tops made of jigsaw pieces, epaulettes replaced by stuffed rats, and headpieces holding flying taxidermy eagles.

It was mania, underpinned by utterly breathtaking clothes that featured embroidered castles, pearlescent party dresses and tailored pantsuits. When the show was seemingly over, the PA blared with the sound of heavy breathing. Models scratched at the windows of the show space, and the four walls of the central box fell to the floor, shattering on impact and revealing a naked Michelle Olley – a performance artist – breathing through tubes and covered in moths that flew free over McQueen's latest creation. The question of whether fashion can ever be art was put to rest that day, as McQueen transcended the role of clothing designer, firmly placing himself among many of the world's greatest contemporary artists.

AUTUMN/WINTER 2006 –
'The Widows of Culloden'

Revisiting his Scottish heritage after the much outrageous, much acclaimed 'Highland Rape' of the early nineties, this show demonstrated McQueen's huge growth as a designer. 'The Widows of Culloden' explored pre-Raphaelite visions of women wandering glens, and a more punkish plaid dress with armour instead of sleeves, all produced with a honed technical ability that resulted in beautiful dresses and sharp tweed suits. The beginning of the show was McQueen's first real foray into technology, with a glass pyramid bringing to life a dancing, floating Kate Moss in the form of a hologram. The audience were silenced as she floated through virtual and physical space in a windblown white Victoriana-style dress, only to disappear in a puff of white smoke.

SPRING/SUMMER 2008 – 'Le Dame Bleu'

The late Isabella Blow became McQueen's muse for this collection, which was shown in Paris and dedicated to her memory. It was a deeply moving collection, designed in collaboration with Blow's other protégé, Philip Treacy. McQueen's previous collection had famously been poorly received, but – perhaps for Issie – this time, he was back on form with bulging hip jackets, fairy-like chiffon dresses and a rainbow-winged gown. It was glorious and full of movement and emotion: the very qualities Issie had always championed, and celebrated, in McQueen.

SPRING/SUMMER 2010 –
'Plato's Atlantis'

By this time, McQueen had become the world's fashion icon – and Lady Gaga's, too. 'Plato's Atlantis' is perhaps one of McQueen's most deified collections: one that fearlessly embraced new technologies that the rest of the fashion industry was perhaps too timid to face head-on. On the day of the show Lady Gaga tweeted that she would be premiering her brand-new single during McQueen's runway show, which fans all over the world could witness by tuning in to a livestream on Nick Knight's groundbreaking website SHOWstudio.

People went online to watch fashion history in motion, prompting so many logins that the site crashed. But the show, as ever, had to go on. What was shown was an amalgam of influences: fish and butterfly prints, drawn from McQueen's adoration of scuba diving, were printed onto stiff fabrics that were nipped and tucked into bulbous tulip skirts and wrapped tightly around torsos. The models became anthropomorphised versions of tropical fish and coral reefs, a thematic evolution for McQueen that dissected humankind's evolution from the seas. Cameras on sliding runners filmed the audience's reaction and projected it onto massive screens that flanked the entrance of the runway. The result was to make the fashion crowd stare at themselves, a favourite trick of the designer's. This was the birth of McQueen's genius armadillo boots, as well as the start of fashion's ever-evolving relationship with technology.

AUTUMN/WINTER 2010 – 'Angels & Demons'

McQueen's suicide in 2010 came just before he was due to present his latest collection, 'Angels and Demons', in Paris. McQueen had left a lasting legacy on the fashion industry, and the wider world, showing artists of all kinds the creative and political potential and influence one person can have. Left behind, too, was a small, delicate collection of sixteen pieces, which would be shown in a small salon in Paris, shared with friends from both within fashion and outside it. For his final ever collection, McQueen looked back: back into beauty, fine craftsmanship, and his own archives. Each dress was draped on a mannequin and had been cut, sewn and pressed by McQueen. Eschewing his prior interest in technology in favour of iconic religious women – whose figures were sewn into the fabrics – McQueen's little-known posthumous collection was a powerful, emotional look at the things he loved best: craft, skill, elegance, tailoring, darkness and light, and, of course, the women whom he dressed. It was tailoring in all its precision, and romanticism in all its beauty and freedom.

04—

McQUEEN THE MAN

McQUEEN THE MAN

McQueen's star had risen. While he was lauded publicly as a fashion genius, behind closed doors McQueen was gentle, cheeky and hard working. Surrounded by a team of brilliant women, incredibly close with his mum, and with a love for escaping to the depths of the seas and the expansive English countryside, McQueen's life outside of fashion shaped what he showed within it. Away from the public eye, however, McQueen battled with addiction and depression, and despite his success, he eventually took his own life. McQueen's is a story of brilliance and tragedy, and while he is remembered for his influence on fashion, he was known to friends and family as a loving, caring, irreplaceable man.

McQueen the Man

"

I DIDN'T PLAN OUT MY LIFE LIKE THAT. WHEN PEOPLE RECOGNISE AND RESPECT WHAT YOU DO, THAT'S NICE, BUT I DON'T THINK YOU EVER DO THIS TO BE FAMOUS. FAME SHOULD BE LEFT TO THE FILM STARS. WE'RE JUST OFFERING A SERVICE.

"

– Alexander McQueen

By the millennium, Alexander McQueen was one of the most well-known, loved and revered designers the fashion industry, and the world, had ever known. This chubby lad from East London had shown the world the darkest, most brilliant depths of his mind, and proven that fashion could be a radical arena for conversation, politics and art.

In 2003, he was named International Designer of the Year, British Designer of the Year – an award he received four times – and was awarded a CBE by Queen Elizabeth II for his contribution to the world of fashion. Just eleven years after he graduated from Central Saint Martins and established a whirlwind friendship with Isabella Blow, McQueen had solidified his position as a true fashion icon.

After shirking his father's expectations that he go into a trade, McQueen went on to stage a brilliant takeover of the global fashion industry. This one man can be credited not only with changing the realm of design during his reign as the Rebel King, but also with shaping today's fashion industry in its embrace of technology, its sociopolitical edge, and its democratisation into a global obsession rather than an elitist profession for a chosen few.

And while McQueen was forever stretching and twisting the puppet strings, smashing the limits and offering fashion a view of its own potential, his personal life was left largely undiscussed. In order to create such change in an industry obsessed with itself, McQueen had to be drawing his influences from somewhere outside of fashion. And indeed he was.

In the early days – as Lee changed to Alexander, and his collections began to make waves across the world – he was exactly the same boy who'd grown up misunderstood, anti-establishment, and always challenging his critics through shock. It was the time of new rave. Ecstasy had just become available and was rip-roaring through the London nightlife scene like no drug had before. It changed music, partying, everything, and – as orchestrated by McQueen – this new age of partying changed fashion, too.

MCQUEEN

While McQueen's days were spent in his small studio in Hoxton, East London – a hub of cheap property and high creativity at the time – his nights were spent with his friends in London's gay heart: Soho.

Populated by prostitutes, drag queens, flamboyant gay men and butch lesbians, McQueen's evenings were often whiled away in the glorious, nihilistic world of gay clubbing, cigarette smoke, drugs and dancing.

It was on these streets that McQueen found a group of misfits with whom he perfectly fit. They would come to his shows and help in the preceding chaos, all sewing, styling and smoking to the last minute. His mum, Joyce, would arrive with plates of sandwiches for everyone as they worked to produce Lee's early masterpieces. It was thrilling, energetic, and like nothing fashion had ever seen.

"

I DON'T WANT TO DO
A COCKTAIL PARTY.
I'D RATHER PEOPLE
LEFT MY SHOW AND
V O M I T E D .
I PREFER EXTREME
REACTIONS. I WANT
HEART ATTACKS.
I WANT AMBULANCES.

"

– Alexander McQueen

By the mid-nineties, McQueen was spending less time with this set, although they still received much of his adoration, as well as some fantastic free clothes. As he rocketed to fashion fame, he found himself spending most of his time with his friend and on-and-off muse, Isabella Blow, at her country estate, Hilles, in Gloucestershire. Here, Isabella offered him lessons in falconry. As a teenager, McQueen had been a keen birdwatcher, and an active member of his high school's ornithologists' club. He had spent his childhood watching birds, and now had a chance to handle them.

McQueen's work in fashion constantly referenced the birds he loved, from his early collection, 'The Birds', to the falcon headdresses seen at 'Voss', to the famous Birds of Paradise dress. Even today, McQueen's take on the swallow forms the central logo of his diffusion line, McQ. Across his career, fashion critics would continue to admire the freedom of movement in his work, a skill McQueen had witnessed in the birds he so adoringly watched over the years.

While McQueen was receiving accolades – and creating outrage – for his fashions, he attracted a set of famous friends. Within a few years he had gone from working for others to working for himself, and had become a leader in his field. He was a favourite of the supers of the nineties – Kate Moss, Sophie Dahl and Naomi Campbell all adored him, eventually becoming close friends outside of the fashion game.

By 1997 McQueen was designing tour costumes for none other than David Bowie. He designed Bowie's entire wardrobe for his 1997 tour, as well as the famed Union Jack jacket, immortalised on the cover of the pop legend's twentieth studio album, *Earthling*.

Before long, the genius Björk had recognised McQueen's talents too, and his designs featured on the cover of her 1997 album *Homogenic*, lensed by the legendary Nick Knight, who would become one of McQueen's biggest collaborators. McQueen eventually directed the video for 'Alarm Call', off the same album, which was also shot by Nick Knight. The video is a trippy journey through a rainforest's river. Björk swims with crocodiles and becomes intimate with snakes as she rafts through vertical bodies of water and grasps for beams of sunlight, her McQueen dress eventually being feasted on by piranhas.

MCQUEEN

And while McQueen's falling in with the in crowd was the beginning of many beautiful friendships, as well as genius artistic collaborations, people later reported that his unbridled success changed him. Coming from a place with little money to having an expense account and a high income, he would readily spend thousands of pounds shopping, and often consumed copious amounts of drugs just to keep himself going.

Yet he always retained a close, loving relationship with his mother, whom he utterly adored. They were a hilarious double act, often bickering and smoking on the sidelines of shows. Although his relationship with other members of his family was somewhat tumultuous, Joyce was always standing, peering with pride, on the sidelines of every show. In an interview where McQueen was interviewed by Joyce, she asked him what makes him proud. He replied, 'You.'

His beloved dogs were another source of grounding among all of this success. McQueen's three pet English bull terriers were like children to him. McQueen absolutely adored his dogs, taking them everywhere. They were rumoured to sleep on Roberto Cavalli cushions, but that's probably just talk. There are countless stories of these three dogs bounding about backstage at every show, with McQueen even bringing two of them onto the runway for his bow after one of his shows.

By the time McQueen joined Givenchy in 1997, he was designing four, sometimes six collections a year. These collections were of an epic scale, and with the world watching his every move – both at Givenchy and at McQueen – each collection, with his growing success, held higher stakes than the last.

But McQueen rose to the challenge time and again, harnessing the evidently expansive limits of his imagination and producing acclaimed collection after acclaimed collection that shocked the press and had the world hooked. McQueen made fashion exciting again, invigorating both fashion and its followers with brand-new perspectives.

These perspectives came from everything around the designer. Aside from birdwatching, McQueen was also an obsessive film fan. Looking across his collections, you can spot countless references to the cinematographic greats. His second collection was inspired by the blood and dirt of Martin Scorsese's iconic *Taxi Driver*. A 2005 collection was based on *Picnic at Hanging Rock*, directed by Peter Weir, and 'The Overlook' collection in 1999 aimed to find a softer side to Kubrick's chilling *The Shining*.

He was obsessed with historical texts, and adored both religious iconoclastic imagery and the women they featured. Each collection was based on something totally outside of fashion, and then applied to a fashion context. In an art form that is supposed to reflect life and society, McQueen was a master at marrying unlikely references – often the historic with the contemporary – and translating them into mind-blowing shows filled to the brim with totally wearable pieces.

MCQUEEN

McQueen was the man who made fashion great, but behind him was a team of dedicated women who helped him realise his wild ideas. Katy England, who is the silent hero of McQueen's great creative success, met McQueen outside his second ever runway show. They instantly clicked, and that spark turned into a house fire. They would go on to work together for over a decade. From the first show she styled – 'The Birds' in 1995 – to when she resigned as creative director of the McQueen brand in 2007, she was his confidante, his second opinion, and his fit model on whom he'd try all his clothes before shows. Katy was a great friend of McQueen's right up until the end of his life and although a lot of attention is shone on McQueen's relationship with Isabella Blow, his friendship with Katy was one of love, quietness, a shared adoration and mutual creativity.

Sarah Burton, who now holds the position of creative director at Alexander McQueen, was McQueen's design protégé. A quiet girl from northern England who grew up wearing her brother's hand-me-downs, she longed for beautiful clothes. After her tutor at Central Saint Martins saw her keen eye for research, she was recommended for a job as McQueen's assistant. 'It was like sculpture – I've never seen anything like it,' she told *Vogue* of McQueen's working process. 'In such a short space of time he did everything. Tailoring, evening-wear, dresses, embroidery, leather, knits – everything!'

Burton learned everything she knew working next to McQueen, by listening, observing and – in the early years – never being able to make a mistake, because there was no money to remake something that had gone wrong. At McQueen's right hand for fourteen years, Burton was his trusted sidekick – and when it came to design, she could do anything he asked of her.

In the year 2000 McQueen got married. His homosexuality wasn't necessarily something accepted by his family. When asked if his newfound fame and fortune had changed their attitudes, he replied, 'No. They haven't always been cool about it. My father was a London taxi driver, and he would come home at night and say, "God I nearly ran over a bloody queer last night," and then all of a sudden everything's hunky dory just because I'm solvent? I can't buy that.'

Nonetheless, McQueen – after a boozy night at the Groucho Club in London with Kate Moss, Annabelle Neilson and his then-boyfriend George Forsyth – planned a wedding. It was before the UK legalised gay marriage, so a few months after the engagement, McQueen and Forsyth boarded a flight to Ibiza, where they were married among a star-studded throng aboard a three-storey yacht.

The yacht was the perfect setting for McQueen's only marriage, for his love of animals – from birds to dogs – also extended to the seas and the creatures within them. Despite the setting, and the fact that the pair were ferociously in love, his marriage to Forsyth lasted little over a year: that ferocity had turned sour, and the pair made one another dreadfully unhappy.

McQueen adored scuba diving, and he spent the latter years of his life exploring the oceans around the Maldives. Perhaps one of McQueen's most successful, celebrated collections was 'Plato's Atlantis'. It was the first time he'd truly brought his love of coral reefs, sea creatures and scuba-diving into his work, and it received unanimous acclaim, remaining one of McQueen's best-selling collections to date.

In these later years McQueen would retire weekly to his cottage, a converted granary in East Sussex with views of the sea and – on a clear night – the sparkling lights of northern France. 'I don't find inspiration there – it gives me a peace of mind. Solitude, and a blank canvas to work from, instead of the distractions of the concrete jungle,' McQueen once said.

Although McQueen was achieving huge critical success, his business at its all-time peak and his income higher than ever, it all came to an end on the morning of 11 February, 2010. At the age of forty, just three years after the tragic suicide of Isabella Blow and nine days after the death of his beloved mother, Joyce, Alexander McQueen took his own life.

While many in the fashion industry had been aware that McQueen struggled with depression, nobody expected such genius to end in such tragedy. That morning, his housekeeper arrived at McQueen's London home to find that the designer had hanged himself with his favourite brown belt. A post-mortem later announced that McQueen had imbibed a cocktail of drugs and slit his wrists with a meat cleaver and a ceremonial dagger.

He left a single note, which read, 'Please look after my dogs. Sorry. I love you. Lee.'

McQueen the Man

The world was in shock, as was his family, who'd had no idea how severely unwell Lee had been. 'If we had known the extent of it, we would have been bashing down doors, but we didn't,' his eldest sister, Janet, said. 'We all spoke to Lee about the drugs, but he was a man in his late thirties. I don't want to name names, I've got to be careful, but people knew his state of mind and his family didn't ... They knew about the other suicide attempts. We didn't.'

A few weeks later, at St Paul's Church in Knightsbridge, London, the high priests of fashion attended an incredibly sombre funeral for the man who had changed fashion, and the world. Along with his grieving family, Naomi Campbell, Kate Moss, Anna Wintour and Stella McCartney sent fashion's rebel king off to take his final bow.

And while McQueen continues to be mourned the world over, his legacy is perhaps the most influential the fashion world has ever witnessed. It is through his clothes, his ideas and his influence that he lives on – and will live on forever.

05—

McQUEEN
THE BRAND

McQUEEN THE BRAND

From McQueen's first collection in 1992, which
he sold in its entirety to Isabella Blow for £5000,
to his multimillion dollar global fashion house,
his eponymous brand Alexander McQueen has
always been lauded and coveted. McQueen's
creativity was big business – he produced
breathtaking collections of impeccably made,
incredibly wearable clothes that women and men
wanted to buy. He was known for his signature
theatrics and showmanship, and revered for his
flawless tailoring, daring cuts and exquisite use
of fabrics. At its core today, years after McQueen's
death, the brand remains true to its founder's
ultimate vision: to offer women the chance to
dress powerfully and beautifully.

"

I CAME TO TERMS
WITH NOT FITTING
IN A LONG
TIME AGO. I NEVER
REALLY FITTED IN.

I DON'T WANT
TO FIT IN.
AND NOW PEOPLE ARE
BUYING INTO THAT.

"

Fashion is nothing without its wearers. A controversial opinion, and one vehemently opposed by fashion aesthetes, is that it doesn't matter how artistic a collection might be – if it doesn't sell, there will be no money to make the next collection.

It's no surprise, then, that many designers focus on creating clothes that are sellable, living radiantly glamorous, all-expenses-paid lives with little artistic integrity. Other designers, who commit solely to art, often find themselves under serious financial strain, forced to abandon their fashion dreams for more profitable pursuits. But not McQueen.

McQueen was art, McQueen was the highest of high-fashion. McQueen used his boundless creativity to make utterly fantastic, brilliantly beautiful and incredibly wearable clothes – clothes people wanted to buy. In his brand, he perfectly balanced art and commerce in a way no other brand had.

From its founding days in the early '90s, the Alexander McQueen brand quickly earned a reputation for its controversial approach to women's fashion, sparking countless cases of genuine outrage across the fashion community. Before long, McQueen had become known for his creative and daring approach to dressing women. He once described women wearing McQueen as 'women to be scared of'.

The house's designer was dubbed 'l'enfant terrible', 'the hooligan of British fashion'. Yet the brand was splashed across magazines and worn by the coolest editors, its shows walked and attended by the crème de la crème of fashion. It was the perfect foundation for any fashion label: daring, controversial, outrageous and beautiful.

While it took years, past the shocking 'Taxi Driver' and 'Highland Rape' collections, the fashion industry eventually saw beyond the showmanship and began to appreciate the clothes themselves. But McQueen continued to court controversy, always pushing the boundaries of what the fashion industry deemed acceptable. In 1998, he cast double amputee Aimee Mullins to walk down the runway on intricately carved wooden legs. The fashion industry called it disempowering, but Mullins and McQueen were proud to have platformed a model with a disability, saying that she had just as much right to a place on the runway as anyone else.

In 1999, the beautiful Shalom Harlow walked onto a rotating platform wearing a giant white dress. Two robotic arms on either side of the platform then sprayed the dress in neon yellow and black lines while an emotional audience watched. Katy England, McQueen's right-hand woman, said that this moment was the only time she ever saw McQueen moved to tears during one of his own shows. It has been described as one of the most profound moments in fashion history, capturing the interplay between aggression and vulnerability, exploring the relationship between our control over technology, and its control over us. The press couldn't decide if it was misogyny or genius.

Season upon season the brand's profile expanded, and the world's excitement skyrocketed. Fashion had never seen anything like it before.

The hype around the brand, and McQueen himself, grew as the designer began to win fashion's highest awards. All through the nineties you could only buy a McQueen piece at selected boutiques and department stores, and the lone McQueen shop in London's West End. These stores became destinations, attracting flocks of shoppers from around the world desperate to snag a piece from the l'enfant terrible of British fashion.

In December 2000, the Gucci group – under the direction of the lauded designer Tom Ford, who had been a big inspiration for McQueen – bought 51 per cent of the brand and appointed Lee as the creative director of Alexander McQueen. This meant Lee, who continued to own 49 per cent of the brand, also kept complete creative control.

This huge, exciting investment saw McQueen terminated from his post at Givenchy, a year before his contract with the fashion house was over. Now he could put all his energies into his eponymous label. After the deal was signed, flagship stores quickly opened across Europe and the United States: in London, Milan, New York, Los Angeles and Las Vegas. Now the brand had spread across the world, and fans could see the clothes they'd adored on the catwalk up close in store.

"

I WANT TO EMPOWER W O M E N . I WANT PEOPLE TO BE SCARED OF THE WOMEN I DRESS.

"

– Alexander McQueen

And in true fashion style, under the guidance of the giant Gucci group, McQueen's shows relocated from London to Paris – the fashion capital of the world – premiering with the 2001 show 'The Dance of the Twisted Bull', an ode to Spanish flamenco and bull-fighting culture, featuring a dress with two huge spears erupting from the back.

THE FRAGRANCES

In January 2003, the noted perfumer Jacques Cavallier approached McQueen about collaborating on a fragrance. The brand's first scent, 'Kingdom', was launched on 17 March the same year – the day of McQueen's birthday. *Vogue* described it as 'a musky-oriental so heavy on the cumin that some hours after spraying, you could mistake it for body odour'. But of course a McQueen fragrance would never be gentle: even in making a fragrance he was disruptive.

THE SKULL SCARF

In the same year, as part of his 'Irere' collection, McQueen launched perhaps the most iconic of all of his brand symbols: the skull scarf. Copied the world over, and emulated by countless other designers, this became perhaps the world's most coveted, most well-worn accessory.

THE MENSWEAR COLLECTION

McQueen was in hot demand. In response to a growing global interest in men's fashion, he designed his first menswear collection in 2005 to critical, and commercial, acclaim.

THE COSMETICS

In 2007 McQueen was the first designer to collaborate with the iconic make-up brand MAC Cosmetics, launching their premier collection of designer make-up. The collection took inspiration from McQueen's Autumn/Winter collection 'The Forgotten', where the models wore zany greens and teals on their eyes with strong slicks of black eyeliner, an homage to Elizabeth Taylor in the elaborate movie *Cleopatra* – long before the years of YouTube tutorials and *RuPaul's Drag Race*. As ever, McQueen was driving fashion into new arenas.

THE MCQ LINE

By 2008 the brand had grown so popular that it made sense for McQueen to launch a second, more affordable line: McQ, which has stores all over the world today. Originally touted as a denim line, the idea was to take the rebellious heart of the Alexander McQueen brand and channel it into more wearable, everyday pieces for his younger, more relaxed fans.

MCQUEEN ONLINE

In the same year, he took Alexander McQueen online in the US, adopting the digital shopping trend long before many other, well-established design houses. McQueen had global reach, and the world was hooked.

This working-class lad made fashion exciting, daring again, and people wanted in. He had achieved the seemingly impossible: he'd mounted the fashion horse and charged the industry, rising as its king. He democratised fashion, demolishing its elitist walls, which sent a thrilling message to the world, to the people who loved fashion but never thought they'd get a look-in.

McQueen had proven it could be done, and more and more people flocked to join the industry, which was growing at an unprecedented rate. McQueen had a huge hand in this expansion, too.

There was eyewear, fragrance, a diffusion line, menswear, womenswear, pre-fall and high-summer collections, make-up, handbags, accessories, and countless stores across the world. This was what global fashion domination looked like, and it was orchestrated masterfully by McQueen.

Alexander McQueen, as both a designer and a brand, fundamentally changed the fashion world. He blurred the lines between politics, art and clothes; manipulated the worldwide press; and boldly embraced technology. He always had his finger on the pulse. Anything the great designer threw at the world would stick, including his other brand collaborations with Samsonite, PUMA and Target.

Beyond his creations, which are a rich, complicated gift to fashion, art and culture, McQueen's brand lives on, continuing to dominate the fashion stage, a brilliant model for other designers the world over. Even after his death, the fashion industry continues to look to him for inspiration.

06—

THE LEGACY

THE LEGACY

When McQueen died, he left behind a fashion industry that was completely different to the one he had entered. He not only built a multimillion dollar global brand and an extensive and impressive oeuvre, he created a new silhouette, revolutionised the idea of a runway show and its audience, and changed the way women dressed. He re-imagined what fashion could be, what it could mean – as fashion, as art, as political comment. But perhaps his most important legacy was that he used the power of fashion to democratise dreams and to challenge how we think and how we live.

From Kate Middleton's (now Princess Catherine, Duchess of Cambridge) royal wedding dress to a smash-hit retrospective exhibition, McQueen's ideas live on. His brand thrives, and his influence can still be seen on runways, in fashion magazines, lecture halls, newspapers and art.

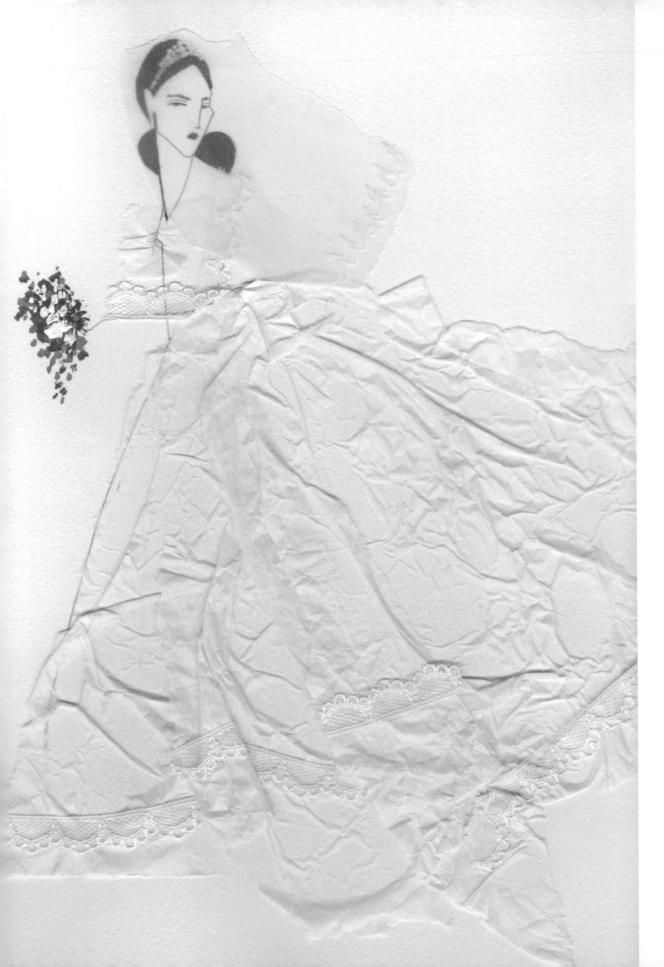

"

WHEN I'M DEAD AND GONE, PEOPLE WILL KNOW THAT THE 21ST CENTURY WAS STARTED BY ALEXANDER MCQUEEN

"

– Alexander McQueen

Alexander McQueen's legacy fulfilled his wishes perfectly: in fashion, everyone knows that the 21st century was started by Alexander McQueen. Fashion is a world that looks in on itself, and it is undoubtable that the fashion masterpieces created by McQueen will be referenced, adored and celebrated for decades to come.

But McQueen's legacy is more than just his fashion. After his tragic death, Alexander McQueen left £50,000 of his £16 million fortune to his dogs to ensure they would be pampered for the rest of their lives. He left £250,000 to each of his siblings, £50,000 each to his godson, nieces and nephews, and long-time housekeepers.

The rest of his estate went to charities. Two of these were dedicated to caring for dogs, another was the Terrence Higgins Trust – an important HIV and AIDS charity in the UK. McQueen also set up a trust fund named the Sarabande Trust, which shares a name with his Spring/Summer 2007 collection. He asked that the trust be used to offer bursaries or grants to students from working-class backgrounds to help them secure a place at university, studying in the creative arts. Although McQueen had by then become accustomed to the luxuries his success afforded him, he hadn't forgotten his beginnings. When McQueen gained his place at Central Saint Martins, if his aunt hadn't lent him the £4,000 course fee, the world may never have witnessed the genius of McQueen.

THE HIPSTER

Beyond his estate, McQueen also left enduring imprints on many parts of the fashion industry, as well as wider culture. McQueen invented, and championed, the low-slung jean silhouette. After he invented the Bumster – estimated to be owned by no more than twenty people in the UK, with a pair selling at auction for a mighty £3500 – the trend of elongating the body by exposing the midriff swept high fashion, as well as the high street, and continues to feature strongly in fashion today as the hipster.

222

A DARKER SIDE OF FASHION

McQueen's exploration of death, darkness and the macabre created collections and clothing that resonated emotionally with people both inside and outside of the fashion industry. Perhaps the most worn piece of McQueen's oeuvre is the skull scarf, which has inspired countless designers and spawned countless counterfeits across the years. Journalist and fashion critic Suzy Menkes once said, 'There was something inside his head and his mind that you didn't want to know about.' While that was true for some, the darkness McQueen expressed across his body of work resonated with many, and also inspired whole movements in music, art and fashion.

The Legacy

WOMEN AS PREDATORS

McQueen graduated from his years on Savile Row with an expert knowledge of cutting and tailoring, which he brought to women's clothing. By reinterpreting classically male codes of dress, introducing severe cutting to his designs, he repositioned the way many women dressed. Although he was often criticised for these designs – with people calling collections, such as 'Highland Rape' misogynistic – many people felt he was actually exploring women as predators, as strong people to be reckoned with. 'They don't look vulnerable,' Professor Claire Wilcox, senior curator of fashion at the Victoria and Albert Museum, once said. 'Actually, they look like they might punch you.'

McQueen often said he was designing armour, and his references always cited strong, persecuted women from history, such as his collection 'Joan', inspired by Joan of Arc, as well as Pope Joan. It was a new move in fashion, one that hadn't been as central to womenswear since Yves Saint Laurent had put his models in suits back in 1966. McQueen surrounded himself with strong women, including his right-hand woman, Katy England, his muse and biggest supporter, Isabella Blow, and his mother, Joyce, whom he adored.

NEW BOUNDARIES FOR BEAUTY

McQueen loved to profile and platform 'unconventional' models. From double amputee Aimee Mullins to performance artist Michelle Olley, who appeared naked as the centrepiece for his controversial 'Voss' show, and who carried significantly more weight than the usual size-zero fashion model. After agreeing to do the show, which has since become one of fashion's most celebrated visuals, Olley wrote the following in her diary:

> *So, diary, why am I doing this? It's not for fashion. I couldn't give a monkey's purple bum about fashion. It's not my friend, denying me access through its gates with bitey little zips, unbending waist measurements and impossible standards. I'm not scared of looking ugly, but public nudity is really not my bag. Why, when McQueen was explaining it, was one half of me screaming 'Yes!' while the other was going 'Arrrrgh – scary!'?*

As scary as it was, McQueen was forever asking his muses to put themselves in different and difficult situations in order to express another side of fashion, of beauty, of life. His fascination with the female form, and with new ways of draping clothes upon it, as well as the symbolism that informed his designs – from Victoriana, to witchcraft, to paganism, to religion, to sex – meant McQueen made countless things that were deemed ugly by society, totally and utterly beautiful.

The Legacy

MCQUEEN

FASHION AS THEATRE AND POLITICS

McQueen entered the ring and significantly changed the world's attitude to fashion, and what could be *in* fashion. Through his shows he discussed provocative topics such as mental illness, decay and death, disability, menstruation, vivisection and the primal nature of humanity. The heralded designer paid homage to the women he designed for by dedicating his life to creating the most beautiful, sensational clothes for them to wear.

McQueen also pioneered fashion's theatrical potential: before him, fashion shows had never been quite so extravagant, visually stimulating or theatrically moving. McQueen built entirely new sets, he added countless new dimensions to the way fashion shows could be presented, he moved audiences to tears and outrage, ultimately using fashion as a means of provocation. Not only did McQueen introduce many new things into fashion, he ingrained them into its nature, raising people's expectations of fashion as a whole, and leaving it as so much more than it had been when he entered.

AND ULTIMATELY, SAVAGE BEAUTY

In May 2011 the Metropolitan Museum of Art in New York opened the doors to one of its most successful exhibitions ever. 'Savage Beauty', curated by Andrew Bolton and Harold Koda, displayed – across countless rooms – the late Alexander McQueen's archive for the world to see. And see it, they did – first via video and imagery taken after fashion's biggest event, the Met Gala, organised by *Vogue* editor Anna Wintour, and then in reality by people who flocked in droves – a staggering 650,000 over three months – to see the life's work of one of fashion's most groundbreaking designers.

The exhibition comprised a comprehensive look through the archives of McQueen's own brand, and also featured pieces from the designer's tenure at Givenchy. It was arranged in six different galleries, each of which tethered multiple collections together in one theme. 'The Romantic Mind' featured McQueen's earlier, more poetic work. 'Romantic Gothic and the Cabinet of Curiosities' focused on McQueen's obsession with all things Victoriana: housed in a giant room across endless shelves and boxes, it featured some of McQueen's most imaginative pieces, from dresses, to jewellery, to headpieces. 'Romantic Nationalism' examined McQueen's exploration of his British and Scottish identity, profiling his finest tailoring and pieces from the controversial, iconic 'Highland Rape' collection – the collection that arguably put McQueen on the map. The journey ended with 'Romantic Exoticism', which deconstructed his view of non-western influences, and 'Romantic Primitivism', analysing McQueen's attempts to integrate fashion, evolution, nature and technology.

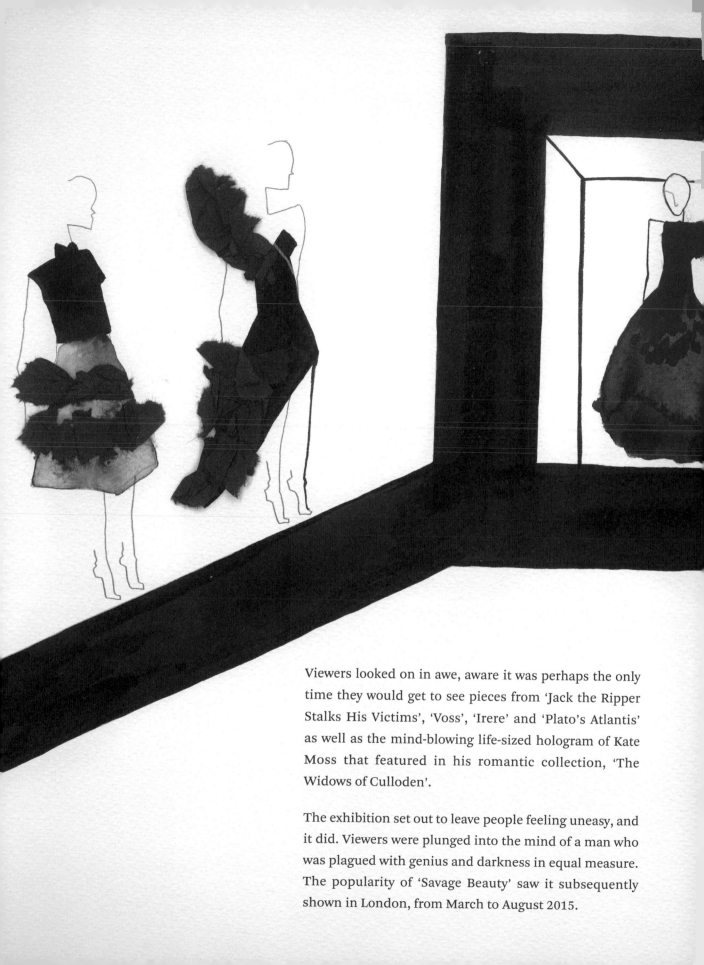

Viewers looked on in awe, aware it was perhaps the only time they would get to see pieces from 'Jack the Ripper Stalks His Victims', 'Voss', 'Irere' and 'Plato's Atlantis' as well as the mind-blowing life-sized hologram of Kate Moss that featured in his romantic collection, 'The Widows of Culloden'.

The exhibition set out to leave people feeling uneasy, and it did. Viewers were plunged into the mind of a man who was plagued with genius and darkness in equal measure. The popularity of 'Savage Beauty' saw it subsequently shown in London, from March to August 2015.

Housed in the great Victoria and Albert Museum, 'Savage Beauty' remains the museum's highest selling show to date, drawing over half a million people through its doors. It was the first time the museum had ever extended its opening hours, and in the final weeks of the show the exhibit stayed open twenty-four hours a day to meet the demand of those anxious to witness the legacy of London's most lauded designer.

But it is impossible to measure a person's legacy through the material things they leave behind. McQueen changed fashion, he altered the way both women and men dress, he established an influential and groundbreaking brand that continues to thrive in the hands of its current creative director, Sarah Burton.

Most of all, however, McQueen left behind proof that anything can be achieved if you work hard and believe that the things in your dreams can become reality. He inspired countless people to enter not only the fashion industry, but also the creative arts more widely. His clothes empowered their wearers. While tragic, McQueen's battle with depression and his eventual suicide stoked the conversation around mental health in the creative arts.

McQueen, both in life and in death, was a renegade, a legend, a true genius and, perhaps most importantly, a person who set out to do something and did it, with passion, vigour and tenacity.

"

SOME DESIGNERS ARE SO AIRY-FAIRY PEOPLE CAN'T CONNECT WITH THEM. I HOPE THAT PEOPLE CAN RELATE TO ME, TO A NORMAL PERSON WHO JUST HAPPENS TO BE A FASHION DESIGNER, THAT PEOPLE CAN TAKE ME AS THEY FIND ME.

"

– Alexander McQueen

Smith Street Books

Published in 2018 by Smith Street Books

Melbourne | Australia
smithstreetbooks.com

ISBN: 978-1-925418-70-5

CIP data is available from the National Library of Australia.

Publisher: Paul McNally
Project manager: Lauren Whybrow
Editor: Vanessa Lanaway
Proofreader: Alison Proietto
Design concept: Murray Batten
Design layout: Heather Menzies, Studio31 Graphics
Illustrator: Rachel Song

Printed & bound in China by C&C Offset Printing Co., Ltd.

Book 54
10 9 8 7 6 5 4 3 2 1

JUN 0 8 2018